Date: 11/17/22

**PALM BEACH COUNTY
LIBRARY SYSTEM**

**3650 Summit Boulevard
West Palm Beach, FL 33406**

Y0-CUO-092

THE HUNT FOR HONEY

by Harriet Brundle

Minneapolis, Minnesota

Credits

All images are courtesy of Shutterstock.com, unless otherwise specified. With thanks to Getty Images, Thinkstock Photo, and iStockphoto.

Front Cover - MuchMania, Mountain Brothers, polygraphus, BigMouse, Philip Kinsey, 2&3 - Nadya_Art, Nikolai Zaburdaev, 6&7 - PowerUp, kosolovskyy, romeocharly62, 8&9 - nata-lunata, 10&11 - Golden Excalibur, Bodgan Denysyuk, 12&13 - shoot4pleasure, Alessandro Cristiano, jongcreative, 14&15 - Piece of Cake, Nata Bene, 16&17 - abi Wolf, Asmodiel, 18&19 - Yuka Kayu, SanderMeertinsPhotography, 20&21 - Magicleaf, Tartila, Reamolko.

Library of Congress Cataloging-in-Publication Data

Names: Brundle, Harriet, author.
Title: The hunt for honey / by Harriet Brundle.
Description: Fusion books. | Minneapolis, MN : Bearport Publishing Company, [2022] | Series: Drive thru | Includes bibliographical references and index.
Identifiers: LCCN 2021011427 (print) | LCCN 2021011428 (ebook) | ISBN 9781647479435 (library binding) | ISBN 9781647479510 (paperback) | ISBN 9781647479596 (ebook)
Subjects: LCSH: Honey--Juvenile literature.
Classification: LCC SF539 .B77 2022 (print) | LCC SF539 (ebook) | DDC 638/.16--dc23
LC record available at https://lccn.loc.gov/2021011427
LC ebook record available at https://lccn.loc.gov/2021011428

© 2022 Booklife Publishing
This edition is published by arrangement with Booklife Publishing.

North American adaptations © 2022 Bearport Publishing Company. All rights reserved. No part of this publication may be reproduced in whole or in part, stored in any retrieval system, or transmitted in any form or by any means, electronic, mechanical, photocopying, recording, or otherwise, without written permission from the publisher.

For more information, write to Bearport Publishing, 5357 Penn Avenue South, Minneapolis, MN 55419. Printed in the United States of America.

CONTENTS

Hop in the Honey Hive 4
The Hunt for Honey 6
At the Hive 8
Beekeepers 10
Gathering the Honey 12
Finishing the Honey 14
Honeycomb 16
Save the Bees 18
Health and Honey 20
Honey Time! 22
Glossary 24
Index 24

HOP IN THE HONEY HIVE

Hello! My name is Lan, and this is my food truck, the Honey Hive! I make yummy snacks with sweet honey. Which one would you like to try?

* MENU *

Honey and orange cookies

Honey cake

Honey bread

Honey taffy

THE HUNT FOR HONEY

Honey is made by honeybees all over the world. The bees make honey from plants.

Flowers have a sweet, sugary **liquid** called **nectar**. Bees suck the nectar out of the plants to make honey.

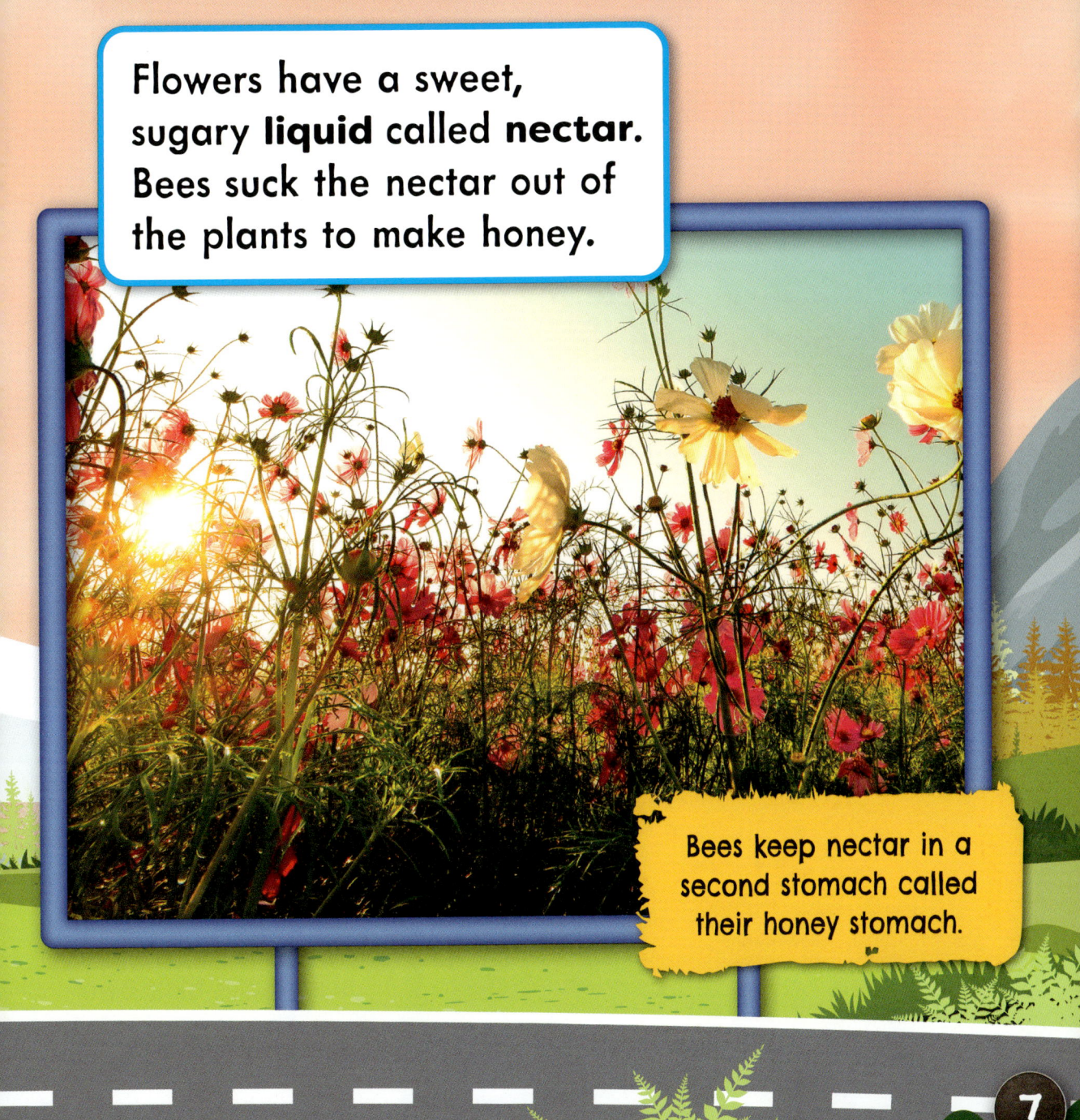

Bees keep nectar in a second stomach called their honey stomach.

AT THE HIVE

After they get the nectar, the bees fly to their hive. At the hive, they pass the nectar from bee to bee.

BEE-MADE HIVE

HUMAN-MADE HIVES

Bees make their own hives. They can also live in human-made hives.

Then, the bees put the nectar in the honeycomb **cells** of their hive. They fan the nectar with their wings to turn it into honey. After that, they cover each cell with **beeswax** to keep the honey inside.

A BEE CLIMBING INTO A HONEYCOMB CELL

BEEKEEPERS

Beekeepers take care of human-made hives. These hives have wooden frames that hold the honeycomb.

Beekeepers make sure the bees in their hives are healthy.

Bees make honey for food. But they often make more than they need. Beekeepers gather the extra honey from the hive.

Honeycomb in a wooden frame

GATHERING THE HONEY

When a beekeeper gathers honey, they may spray smoke on the bees. This stops the bees from stinging.

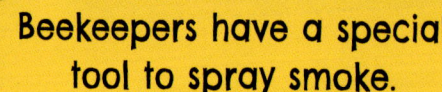

Beekeepers have a special tool to spray smoke.

Then, the beekeeper takes the frames out of the hive and cuts wax off of the honeycomb cells.

A beekeeper uses a knife to cut the wax from the honeycomb.

FINISHING THE HONEY

Next, the frames are put into a machine that spins them around. This makes the honey come out of the cells.

Honeycomb frame in a machine

The finished honey will look golden and taste sweet!

The honey may be **filtered** to make sure there is no wax in it. Then, the honey is done! It is packed up and sold.

HONEYCOMB

Some beekeepers also sell honeycomb for people to eat. They cut the honeycomb out of the frame with the honey still in it.

HONEYCOMB

Honeycomb can be eaten on its own or added to other things.

17

SAVE THE BEES

As they make honey, bees **pollinate** plants. Plants provide much of the food we eat.

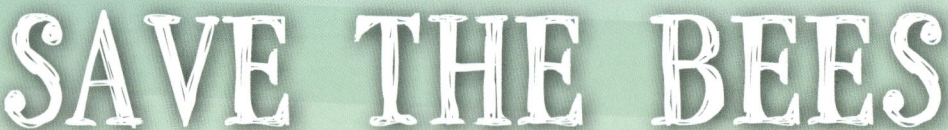

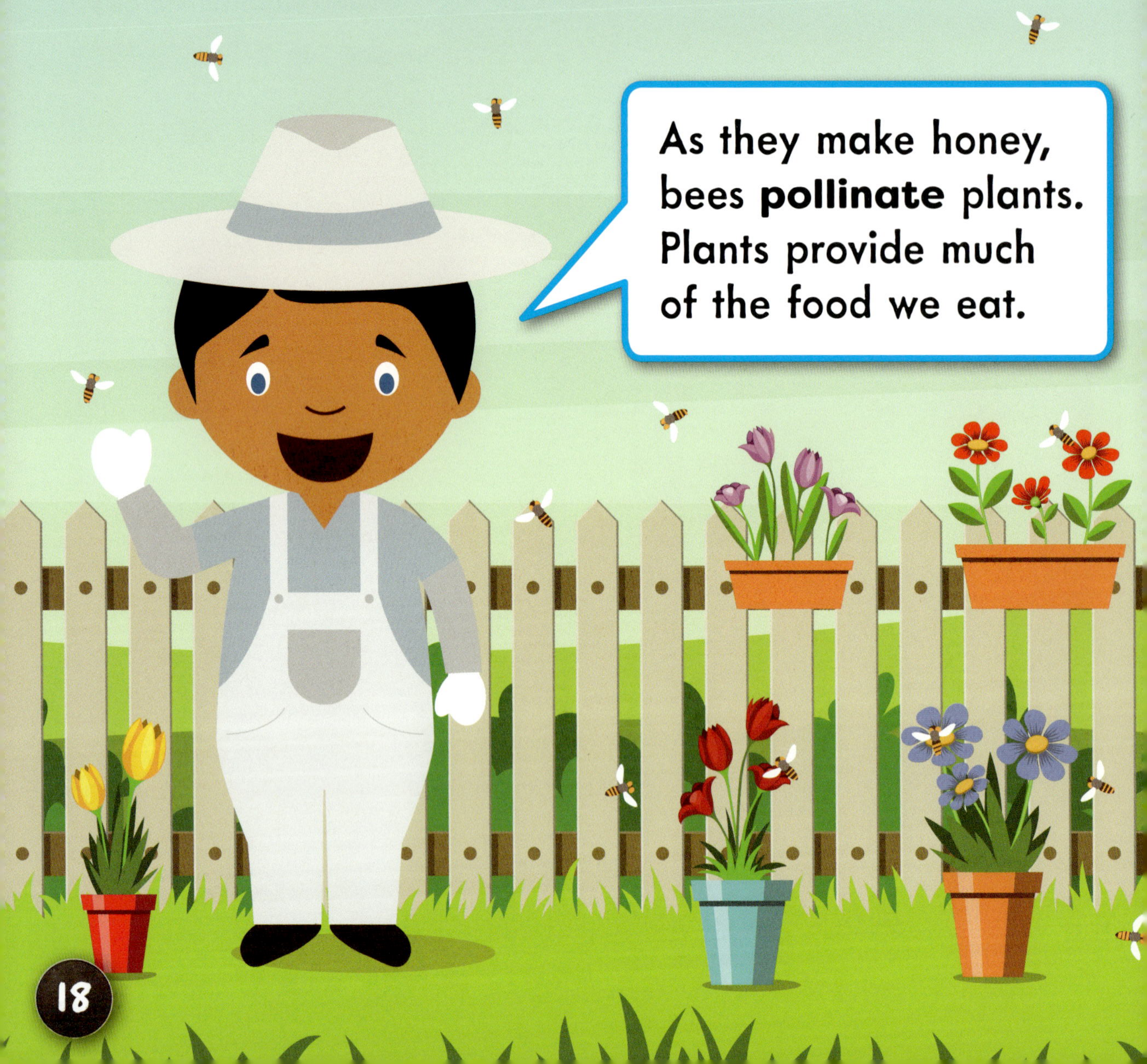

But the number of bees in the world is getting lower. This is because people have **destroyed** some of the places where bees live. You can help save the bees by taking care of nature.

One way to help bees is to plant a garden for them!

HEALTH AND HONEY

Taking care of bees means we can keep using their honey. Some people like to use honey when they are sick.

A warm cup of water with honey and lemon can make a sore throat feel better.

HONEY TIME!

Hooray! We've made it back with lots of honey. Now, I can make more sweet treats.

The Honey Hive

* MENU *

Honey and orange cookies

Honey cake

Honey bread

Honey taffy

GLOSSARY

beeswax a yellow substance that is made by bees and used to build their honeycombs

cells very tiny parts of something larger

destroyed ruined or harmed completely

filtered to have been cleaned by removing small bits

liquid a thing that flows, such as water

nectar a sweet liquid found in flowers that is used by bees to make honey

pollinate to take pollen from one plant to another so that new plants will grow

INDEX

beekeepers 10–13, 16
bees 6–12, 18–20
hives 8–11, 13
honeycomb 9–10, 13–14, 16–17
nectar 7–9
plants 6–7, 18–19